P r e s e n t e d   t o

....

F r o m

....

D a t e

....

WRITTEN BY JONI EARECKSON TADA

You've Got a Friend

Illustrations by Jeff Meyer

CROSSWAY BOOKS · WHEATON, ILLINOIS

A DIVISION OF GOOD NEWS PUBLISHERS

PUBLISHER'S ACKNOWLEDGMENT

The publisher wishes to acknowledge that the text for *You've Got a Friend* appeared originally as "The Weight of Two Worlds" in *Tell Me the Truth,* written by Joni Eareckson Tada with Steve Jensen and illustrated by Ron DiCianni. Special thanks to Ron DiCianni for the idea and vision behind the creation of the series. For more stories in the "Tell Me" series, *Tell Me the Story, Tell Me the Secrets,* and *Tell Me the Promises,* all published by Crossway Books, are available at your local bookstore.

You've Got a Friend
Copyright © 1999 by Joni Eareckson Tada
Illustrations ©1999 by Jeff Meyer
Published by Crossway Books
a division of Good News Publishers
1300 Crescent Street
Wheaton, Illinois 60187

Illustrations by Jeff Meyer
Design by David Uttley Design
First printing 1999
Printed in the United States of America

LIBRARY OF CONGRESS CATALOGING-IN-PUBLICATION DATA

Tada, Joni Eareckson.
You've got a friend/text by Joni Eareckson Tada; illustrated by Jeff Meyer.
p. cm.
Appeared originally as "The weight of two worlds in 'Tell me the truth.'"
Summary: Benjamin, sad and lonely in his wheelchair, receives help from two angels when they create the opportunity for him to fix his old friend Tony's flat bicycle tire.
ISBN 1-58134-060-5 (hc.: alk. paper)
[1. Friendship Fiction. 2. Angels Fiction. 3. Wheelchairs Fiction. 4. Physically handicapped Fiction. 5. Bicycles and bicycling Fiction.] I. Meyer, Jeff (Jeffrey D.), ill. II. Title.
PZ7.T116Yo 1999
[Fic]—dc21   99-20931
                                                            CIP

08   07   06   05   04   03   02   01   00   99

15   14   13   12   11   10   9   8   7   6   5   4   3   2   1

For my friend,

the *real* Ben Brewer

NEVER WAS THERE a more gorgeous day on Maple Street. The sky was bright and blue, and leaves on the trees rustled in the breeze. It was the perfect day for playing outside. But it wasn't perfect for Benjamin Brewer. That's because Ben felt like he didn't have a friend in the world. He sat on his big front porch overlooking the street, leaning his head on his hand and watching kids on the far sidewalk toss a Frisbee.

Whoosh! The path of the Frisbee went haywire, and it came sailing into the Brewers' front yard. Thump! It hit a tree and fell against the trunk. Ben's heart began to race. He straightened in his chair, as if to spring up and run for the Frisbee.

But try as he would, his legs wouldn't move. As usual, he was stuck in his wheelchair. His shoulders slumped with embarrassment when little Nathan Thompson stopped at the edge of the yard and asked, "Can I get my Frisbee back?"

Ben pretended he hadn't seen it hit the tree. "Huh? Oh, sure, go ahead," he said with a wave of his hand. He then angled his wheelchair away from the boy, who ran into the yard and picked up the Frisbee.

The game started again across the street, and Ben turned his chair to watch. Oh, how he wished his legs worked! He looked down at his clean, unscuffed Nikes. *A lot of good a pair of running shoes does me!* he thought. They looked as new now as they did when he got them a few months ago. *I hate this stupid wheelchair. I can't do anything. I can't play Frisbee. I can't ride my bike anymore . . . and I don't have any friends like I used to—not even Tony. It's not fair!*

At that moment, at the other end of the porch (and yet an entire world away), Benjamin was being watched by two special friends, Zoe and Astor. Zoe, who was sitting on the railing, shook his head and sighed, "That little guy sure could use a good friend right now. He needs to know God's love."

The other nodded in agreement. Although angels like Zoe and Astor could not feel sadness the same way humans did, it was obvious to anyone that Benjamin was very unhappy.

Finally Astor piped up, "I'm glad the Master sent us here to cheer Ben up. It won't be an easy job. Wheelchairs never are——"

"But," Zoe interrupted as he hopped off the railing and smiled, "that wheelchair will give the Master a chance to show His love and power."

"This I have to see," said Astor. It's not that this angel was doubtful; he had great faith in God. It's just that he didn't know as much as Zoe, the more experienced angel who had seen the Master's blueprint for Benjamin's life.

Honka! Honka! It was Tony, Ben's next-door neighbor, on his brand-new red bike. Tony made a big figure eight in front of Ben's house. Zoe elbowed Astor. "See that kid? You'd never guess, but he could use a good friend right now, too. His dad's away a lot on business, and his mother is busy with his new baby sister. He doesn't play with the other kids in the neighborhood. He may look okay on the outside, but he's hurting almost as much as Benjamin on the inside."

"So what do we do with these two boys?" Astor asked. "How do we— ouch!" The angel had leaned against the porch railing. He reached behind him and pulled a nail from the wood. Angels didn't always feel pain like humans, but a heavenly assignment that involved earth sometimes included risks. Astor held the nail up and frowned.

"This is how we do it," said Zoe as he took the nail from Astor's hand.

Just then Tony finished his figure eight and called, "Hey, Ben, I'm going to be in the big bike race on Saturday. Wanna come?"

Ben waved back and shouted, "Sure, Tony, maybe I will!"

The two angels knew from the look on Benjamin's face that he didn't really mean it; his sad smile said it all. They could tell—and maybe even Tony could tell—that Ben *wanted* to go see the neighborhood bike race, but that he'd probably just stay on his front porch.

Zoe sighed at Ben. He sighed at Tony, too, as he watched him wave good-bye and speed down the street. *There's a lot of work to do here,* he thought. *These two boys really need each other.*

Meanwhile, as Tony turned the corner from Maple onto Vine Street, he suddenly felt sad. He remembered that this was the exact spot where Ben had been hit by a car last summer. He had passed this corner hundreds of times without giving Ben's accident a thought. But today was different. He wished Ben and he could race their bikes around the neighborhood the way they used to.

Tony stopped for a moment, balancing his bike with his foot against the curb. *Dear Lord, I wish I could be a better friend to Ben,* he prayed. *We were best friends before the accident. But how do you play with someone in a wheelchair?* Tony almost turned around, but he felt afraid—afraid that he might be embarrassed and not know what to say, afraid that he might make Ben feel bad that he couldn't ride a bike anymore. *Besides,* he thought, *I'm not a good friend—especially for someone like Ben.* And so Tony sighed and went on his way.

Astor's face scrunched up in a question. "Why didn't you stop Tony?" he asked.

Zoe shook his head. "I can't make humans do what they don't want to do. But don't worry," he added. "There is something we can do."

Saturday morning came and with it all the excitement you'd expect over a neighborhood bike race. A few kids were already zooming up and down Maple Street on their bikes, testing their turns and their brakes. Ben rolled his wheelchair out onto his front porch right after breakfast. Watching everyone do wheelies and figure eights made his eyes fill. He sniffed back tears.

Suddenly from several blocks away, a voice making announcements came over a loudspeaker. It wouldn't be long now before the bike race began. Everyone on a bicycle headed down the street. Ben sighed and started to turn around and wheel toward the front door.

Just as he was about to go back inside, he glanced over the side railing of the porch toward Tony's house. Then he gasped. Tony's new red bike was lying on the lawn. And Tony was sitting on his front steps, rubbing his eyes. Ben could tell that something was terribly wrong. Forgetting about everything, he wheeled down the ramp by the side of his driveway.

"What's the matter?" he called when he got to the driveway. "I thought you'd be headed for the starting line with the others."

"My bike tire has a big hole in it," said Tony. Ben could tell that Tony had a big lump in his throat too.

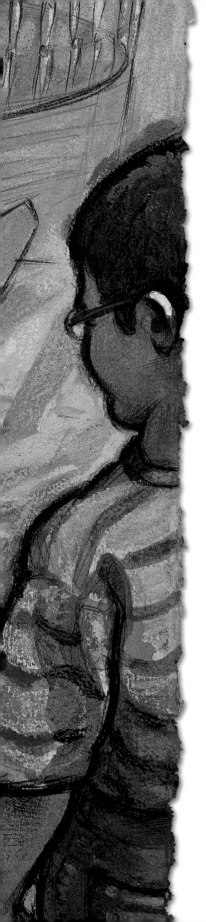

"How'd it happen?" Ben asked as he wheeled closer.

"Who knows? And who cares? My dad is out of town, and Mom says she can't leave my baby sister to take me to the gas station to get it fixed before the race."

Zoe and Astor, who had been listening from their regular spot on the porch, held their breath. This was the big moment. They would now find out if their plan would succeed.

For the first time in many weeks Benjamin's face broke out into a big, broad smile. "Hey, cheer up," he told Tony. "I know what to do. Come on, grab your bike and follow me!"

Zoe and Astor followed the boys, eager to see what would happen.

A very surprised Tony had to trot to keep up with Ben as they hurried toward the Brewers' garage. Ten minutes later, the two of them were remounting the tire on Tony's bike.

Tony stood back and shook his head in amazement. "I can't believe it's fixed! How did you ever learn to patch a tire so quickly?"

"Aw, it's easy once you've had some practice," said Ben. "My wheelchair gets a flat every now and then, and since I really need it to get me to school and church—well,—everywhere, I have to know how to keep this thing in tip-top shape." He grinned and slapped the armrest of his chair.

Zoe and Astor looked at each other in amazement. Neither angel had ever heard Benjamin say anything good about his wheelchair. Not since he got it. Not ever! The angels gave each other a high five.

"It sure helped this morning. Thanks a lot!" said Tony.

"Well, you'd better get going, or you'll be late for the race. Hey, where's the finish line?"

"In front of the courthouse. Are you gonna come?"

Ben smiled. "Don't you think the winner's mechanic should be at the finish line?"

Astor swung his arm around his fellow angel's shoulder and held up a small object, his face beaming. "Who would have thought a nail from a wooden porch railing would fit so wonderfully into the Master's blueprint for Benjamin's life?"

"And not just Benjamin's life," said Zoe. "I think Tony's life will be different now too." The angels stood back and watched to see exactly how the story for both boys would end.

Tony and Ben could hear another call for the race over the distant loudspeakers. If Tony was going to get to the starting line, he had to hurry. But something more powerful than the pull of the race gripped him. He looked at Ben, sitting there in his wheelchair with dirt and grease on his jeans and face, smiling with a wrench in one hand and a rag in the other. It didn't seem to matter to Tony that his dad wasn't there or that his mom couldn't leave to watch him. His friend Ben could. And that made him happier than he'd been for a while.

Tony swung his leg high over the seat of the bike and then stopped before taking off. "You know, it would be great to win the race, but something even better than that already happened today!"

"What's that?" asked Ben.

"I found out that we're still best friends!"

Ben couldn't keep from smiling. He waved to Tony as he turned the corner on his red bike. It was then that Ben said out loud, "The best of friends." And then he took off to find a great spot at the courthouse.